A

ANNA is **for** **BELLE**

By TASHA TUDOR

NEW YORK   HENRY Z. WALCK, INC.   1954

J
T

To dearest
Muff
and
Aunt Middle Mary

A is for Annabelle

Grandmother's doll

B for her Box

on the chest in the hall

C for the Cloak

we take out with care

D for the Dresses

we want her to wear

E for her Earrings

so quaint and so small

F for her Fan

to use at the ball

G for her Gloves

GANTS
DE MA POUPÉE

made of fine leather

H is her Hat

with an elegant feather

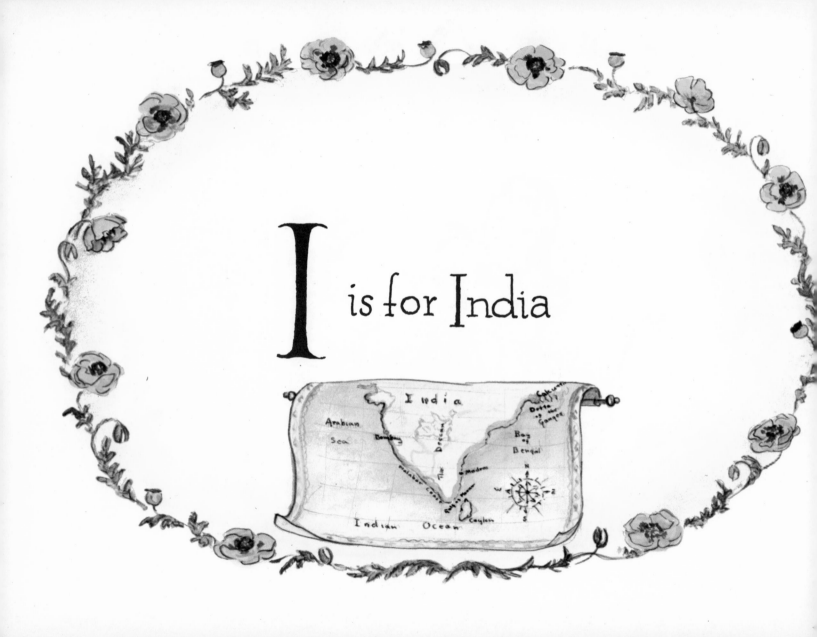

I is for India

whence came her shawl

J is the Jacket

she wears in the fall

K is for Kerchiefs

both frilly and plain

L for the Locket

she wears on a chain

M is her Muff

so warm and so cosy

N is a Nosegay

a bright fragrant posy

O is her Overskirt

worn with such grace

P for her Parasol

all trimmed with lace

Q is the Quilt

which covers her bed

R for the Ribbons

she ties 'round her head

S for her Slippers

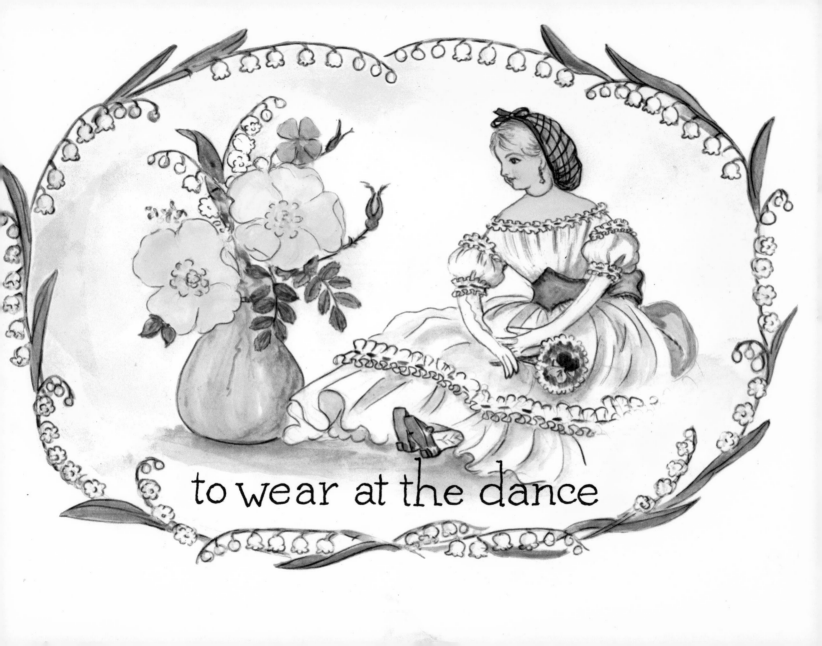

to wear at the dance

T for her Tippet

the latest from France

U for Umbrella

with jet handle on it

V for the Veil

she wears with her bonnet

W—her Watch

to tell her the time

X is the letter

X is for Xerxes

The King

for which I've no rhyme

Y is the Yarn

her stockings to mend

Z is her Zither

and this is the end.